OUTDOOR EXPLORER

I SEE TREES

by Tim Mayerling

TABLE OF CONTENTS

tadpole
books

I SEE TREES

trunk

Trees have trunks.

Trees have bark.

branch

Trees have branches.

twig

Trees have twigs.

Trees have needles.

Trees have leaves.

Trees have flowers.

fruit

Trees have fruit.

nut

Trees have nuts.

seed

Trees have seeds.

Trees have roots.

Trees have nests.

Trees have holes.

Trees have homes.

WORDS TO KNOW

bark   flowers   fruit

leaves   needles   seeds

INDEX

16